The Lucky Yak

by Annetta Lawson
illustrated by Allen Say

Parnassus Press Oakland California
Houghton Mifflin Company Boston 1980

A PARNASSUS PRESS BOOK

Library of Congress Cataloging in Publication Data

Lawson, Annetta.
  The lucky yak.

  SUMMARY: Edward, a yak who has everything, is not
happy until a weekend spent babysitting the overactive
daughter of his analyst teaches him how to find happiness.
  [1. Yaks—Fiction]   I. Say, Allen.   II. Title.
PZ7.L43823Lu   [E]   80-15083
ISBN 0-395-29523-8 (Houghton Mifflin)

This is a story about a yak. If you don't know what a yak is, don't worry. Someone who does know is sure to speak up and say, "Hmmmm. Tibetan beast of burden with long, silky hair." Then you can smile as if you knew it all along.

Actually, this particular yak did not live in Tibet because when he was very young his parents immigrated to America. They wanted a good life for their son, so they scraped together a little money and sailed in great discomfort to the Land of Freedom and Opportunity.

They landed in New Yak which was busy, noisy and confusing. For a time they felt despondent and wondered where all the Freedom and Opportunity were to be found.

At last they met a friendly taxi driver who told them about a town out west called Yakima. This sounded promising, so they bought a map and headed west.

Yakima turned out to be just the place for them. They found work and a little house. They were able to send their young son Edward to school and give him a good education.

Edward Yak had a head for business. When he graduated from school he opened a small restaurant which he called Yak-in-the-Box.

Edward worked hard and his restaurant was a great success. In a few years he opened another and another. Soon he had a chain of restaurants across the country and lots of money was pouring in.

Edward was able to provide for his parents in handsome style. He retired from business and found himself with everything his heart desired, but with nothing much to do.

He tried sports, but a yak
doesn't cut much of a figure
on the tennis court,

and while he liked swimming,
his hair kept clogging up
the swimming pool.

He took a few painting lessons,
but he had no eye for color,

so he tried music, only to
learn that he was tone deaf.
Edward liked to picture himself

at the wheel
of a sleek, fast car, but
he soon found that the
noise made his head ache
and the dust made his eyes water.

In desperation he took up macramé,
but he kept weaving his beard
into the design and it was
discouraging to have to
keep unraveling it.

At this point Edward became depressed and miserable. One of his friends suggested that he see a psychologist and try to get his head together.

He looked in the yellow pages of the Yakima telephone book under "Psychologists." There he read:

Puffin, Huffin N., PhD JD MD DPhil (Oxon) *911-0001*

Thinking that Oxon meant the doctor was an ox, and so could understand a yak's problems, he made an appointment for a week from Thursday, to see Dr. Huffin N. Puffin.

When Edward was shown into Dr. Puffin's office, you may imagine his dismay to discover that the doctor was a puffin and not an ox, but he decided he had gone too far to back out now.

"Mr. Yak," began Dr. Puffin, "just lie back, put your feet up, relax, and tell me what is troubling you."

"Well, Dr. Puffin, I have everything my heart desires: a home in the country, an apartment in the city, and a condominium at Tahoe. I have three classic cars, my own jet and a yacht. I have been around the world several times. But somehow it isn't enough." A tear slid down the yak's nose and dropped onto his ultrasuede vest.

"There just doesn't seem to be any reason to get up in the morning." Another tear slipped down his hairy cheek.

"Hmmmm," said Dr. Puffin. "Hmmmm. Mmmmm. I hear you Mr. Yak. I hear you and I can relate. First and most important you must Hope and you must Believe that things will work out for you. Do you Hope? Do you Believe?"

"Doctor, I do Hope! I do Believe!" cried Edward, for he was greatly impressed by Dr. Puffin's quick analysis of the problem, and also by the way he said, "Hmmmm. Mmmmm."

"Hmmmm. Mmmmm," repeated Dr. Puffin. "I hear you. Now, for a case as serious as yours, I need quiet surroundings while I form a Plan. Mrs. Puffin and I will go to our beach house for a few days. We'll need a sitter for little Muffin Puffin who is two and a half. I don't suppose you've done any puffin-sitting?"

"Well, no . . . ."

"Hmmmm. Mmmmm. I hear you. My dear Mr. Yak, I believe you would be a natural puffin-sitter. You seem to be qualified in every way to care for Muffin. Mrs. Puffin and I will leave tomorrow morning at 8:30. Here is our home address."

At 8:30 Friday morning, Edward rang the bell of Dr. Puffin's house.

Dr. Puffin himself answered the doorbell. "Hmmmm. Mmmmm! Mr. Yak! I am eager to begin a study of your case; Mrs. Puffin and I must be off. Here is a complete set of instructions. Have a good day!"

"But . . ." began Edward.

"I hear you! Remember, Believe! Hope! Hmmmm. Mmmmm!" Dr. Puffin's voice faded as his car rolled away.

"Hm. Mm," tried Edward, but it sounded timid. He set out to find Muffin Puffin.

Finding Muffin was easy; Edward just followed the sounds of great crashes and bangs which were shaking the house. In a large, sunny room he found a small puffin who was throwing her books and toys, one by one, at the wall.

"Good morning, Muffin," said Edward.

"Don't want it!!" screamed Muffin, throwing a block at him. Her aim was excellent.

The yak rubbed a sore nose as he suggested, "Would you like some breakfast?"

"Don't want it!!" roared Muffin.

"All right, we'll play for a while."

"Want breakfast! Do want breakfast!" shrieked Muffin.

They went to the kitchen and Edward started to make some oatmeal.

"Want eggs!" demanded Muffin.

Edward got some eggs.

"Don't want it! Want banana!!"

Edward got a banana.

"Don't want it! Want toast!!"

Edward got bread.

"Don't want it! Want milk!!"

"It's not easy being a natural puffin-sitter," thought the yak.

By lunchtime Friday, Muffin Puffin had taken all the pots and pans out of the cupboards and played drums with them. She had broken a bottle of vinegar and smeared the

kitchen floor with butter. She had applesauce in her feath-
ers. She had fallen and skinned her beak and she had made
a dent in the refrigerator with her tricycle.

"This is going to be a long weekend," thought Edward.

By dinnertime Saturday,
Muffin Puffin had taken the
stuffing out of her teddy-
bear, scribbled on her
stomach with felt pens,

eaten a bar of soap,
flushed her toothbrush down
the toilet, pulled the
leaves off the Boston fern,

and poured a jar of honey into the stereo.
"Hmmm . . . Mmmm . . .
I Believe . . ." said Edward,
but he sounded tired.

By 2:00 Sunday afternoon,
Muffin Puffin had eaten two
crayons, painted the living
room wall with catsup,

hit Edward's sore nose
with a wooden spoon,
filled her shoes
with orange juice,

fallen downstairs, and
screamed "Don't want it!!"
973 times.

Edward telephoned Dr. Puffin's beach house. "Dr. Puffin, you'd better come home," he said.

"I hear you, Mr. Yak," said Dr. Puffin. "We'll be there tomorrow. How is Muffin?"

"She is coloring my right horn green," said Edward.

"I can relate," said Dr. Puffin. "Hmmmm. Mmmmm."

On Monday morning Dr. and Mrs. Puffin returned. "Mr. Yak, I have a Plan!" began Dr. Puffin.

"Doctor, I don't need a Plan. I need to go home," said Edward. "I need to wash the applesauce out of my fur and clean the crayon off my horns. I need a quiet lunch, an afternoon stroll, and a peaceful evening reading a good book. I want my old life, Dr. Puffin. It's a good life and I'm going to enjoy it."

"Hmmmm. Mmmmm. Very good news indeed Mr. Yak! I hear you saying that your problems are solved and that you intend to live happily ever after! Hmmmm. You see how our troubles have a way of disappearing when we Believe and Hope, and most of all when we see how lucky we really are!"

"Hmmmm. Mmmmm," said Edward Yak. And he really meant it.